A VERY NUTTY CHRISTMAS

WINDMILL BOOKS™

BY JODY HILDRETH

Published in 2024 by Windmill Books,
an Imprint of Rosen Publishing
2544 Clinton Street, Buffalo, NY 14224

All photos by Jody Hildreth

Photo credits: Cover (background), series art (string of lights) Dominik Hladik/Shutterstock.com

Cataloging-in-Publication Data

Names: Hildreth, Jody.
Title: A very nutty Christmas / Jody Hildreth.
Description: New York : Windmill Books, 2024. | Series: Nutty celebrations
Identifiers: ISBN 9781538394977 (pbk.) | ISBN 9781538394984 (library bound) | ISBN 9781538394991 (ebook)
Subjects: LCSH: Christmas–Juvenile fiction. | Nuts–Juvenile fiction.
Classification: LCC PZ7.1.H553 Ve 2024 | DDC [E]–dc23

Printed in the United States of America

CPSIA compliance information: Batch #CSWM24: For further information contact Rosen Publishing, New York, New York at 1-800-237-9932

Find us on

It's the morning before Christmas. A package arrives for the Oakenfield family.

Christmas Tree

Fragile

It's their family Christmas tree!

3

Dad looks at the instructions while Forrest inspects the pieces.

Dad says, "This should be easy! We'll be done in no time."

4

Oops!

After a whole morning of work, the tree is upside down.
"Those instructions might be in a different language,"
Dad says, frustrated.

5

Dad says, "Forget about this artificial tree! This year, we will put up a real one."

With a trusty ax, Dad and Forrest are off to find the perfect tree. There's still enough time left in the day.

Whee!

Success! They find the perfect tree in the woods.
And Forrest gets a free ride back to the house.

Dad and Forrest bring the tree home.

Mom is in a festive mood as she decks the halls.

The tree looks perfect, and it is right side up! Even Nutmeg the cat is admiring the tree's beauty.

What a perfect moment. Nothing could possibly go wrong.

But what's that hiding in the tree?

The hungry cat thinks
it looks like dinner!

He pounces!

Poor Dad!

This is turning out to
be tougher than
he thought.

But there is still plenty of the day left to get this tree
decorated before Santa arrives tonight.

Time to get the big box of decorations.

Unfortunately, Dad didn't see
Nutmeg taking a nap on
the floor.

"What a troublemaker that cat is!" says Dad.

Luckily, none of the ornaments were made of glass. They were made of things the Oakenfields collected in the woods throughout the years like acorns, pine cones, and berries.

First thing's first. Forrest thinks it would be a bright idea to check the lights to make sure they all work.

15

Dad starts to put the lights up, just as the room grows darker.

"Better hurry, Dad. It looks like the sun is setting," says Forrest, sipping his hot cocoa.

Forrest spent hours threading winterberries onto string.

Now, he proudly hangs the garland.
Dad inspects the freshly baked Christmas cookies. Yum!

17

But wait—it's getting late! No time to stop and smell the cookies.

Dad needs to hang the ornaments up fast.

He throws them to Mom and Forrest just as fast as he can.

Nutmeg thinks this is all a silly game!

19

And now for the final decoration—the star.
Forrest found this during the summer while visiting the ocean.

Mom says, "This star gives me hope for the new year."

The tree looks beautiful, just in time for bed.

Time to get a family portrait in front of their hard work.
Even Nutmeg joins in.

One more thing left to do before Santa comes! Forrest loads a table with cookies, hot cocoa, and of course a letter telling Santa what he would like for Christmas.

To Santa
North Pole

He winks at Nutmeg.

Once the Oakenfields are in bed, Santa arrives with his big bag.

He quickly leaves the presents and samples some of the cookies and cocoa. Then it's off to another house.

On Christmas morning,
Forrest runs to the tree.
He opens up a big box.

Santa delivered the purrrrfect present— another cat! "I'll name him Jingle," says Forrest.

Dad says, "I wonder what trouble this present will cause!"